THE TWELVE

Days of

CHRISTMAS

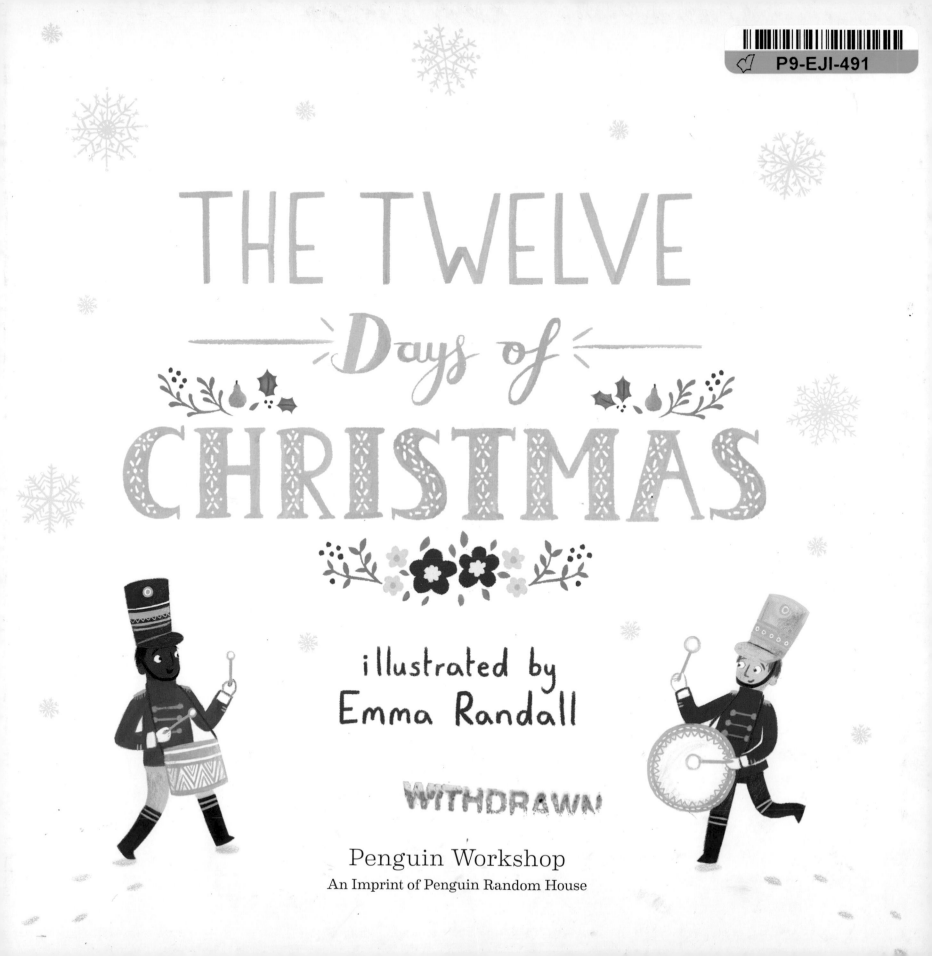

illustrated by
Emma Randall

Penguin Workshop
An Imprint of Penguin Random House

On the first day of Christmas
my true love gave to me
a partridge in a pear tree.

On the second day
of Christmas
my true love gave to me
two turtledoves
and a partridge
in a pear tree.

On the third day of Christmas
my true love gave to me
three French hens,
two turtledoves,
and a partridge in a pear tree.

On the fourth day
of Christmas
my true love gave to me
four calling birds,
three French hens,
two turtledoves,
and a partridge in a pear tree.

On the fifth day
of Christmas
my true love gave to me
five golden rings,
four calling birds,
three French hens,
two turtledoves,
and a partridge
in a pear tree.

On the sixth day of Christmas
my true love gave to me
six geese a-laying,
five golden rings,
four calling birds,
three French hens,
two turtledoves,
and a partridge in a pear tree.

On the seventh day of Christmas
my true love gave to me
seven swans a-swimming,
six geese a-laying,
five golden rings,
four calling birds,
three French hens,
two turtledoves,
and a partridge
in a pear tree.

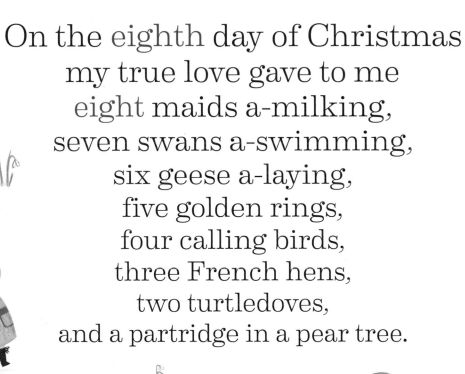

On the eighth day of Christmas
my true love gave to me
eight maids a-milking,
seven swans a-swimming,
six geese a-laying,
five golden rings,
four calling birds,
three French hens,
two turtledoves,
and a partridge in a pear tree.

On the ninth day of Christmas
my true love gave to me
nine ladies dancing,
eight maids a-milking,
seven swans a-swimming,
six geese a-laying,
five golden rings,
four calling birds,
three French hens,
two turtledoves,

and a partridge in a pear tree.

On the tenth day of Christmas
my true love gave to me
ten lords a-leaping,
nine ladies dancing,
eight maids a-milking,
seven swans a-swimming,
six geese a-laying,
five gold rings,
four calling birds,
three French hens,
two turtledoves,

and a partridge in a pear tree.

On the eleventh day of Christmas
my true love gave to me
eleven pipers piping,
ten lords a-leaping,
nine ladies dancing,
eight maids a-milking,
seven swans a-swimming,
six geese a-laying,
five golden rings,
four calling birds,
three French hens,
two turtledoves,

and a partridge in a pear tree. ♫

On the twelfth day of Christmas
my true love gave to me
twelve drummers drumming,
eleven pipers piping,
ten lords a-leaping,
nine ladies dancing,
oight maids a-milking,
seven swans a-swimming,
six geese a-laying,
five golden rings,
four calling birds,
three French hens,
two turtledoves . . .

and a partridge
in a pear tree.

To Max, my true love x

PENGUIN WORKSHOP
Penguin Young Readers Group
An Imprint of Penguin Random House LLC

Illustrations copyright © 2017 by Emma Randall. All rights reserved. Published by Penguin Workshop, an imprint of Penguin Random House LLC, 345 Hudson Street, New York, New York 10014. PENGUIN and PENGUIN WORKSHOP are trademarks of Penguin Books Ltd, and the W colophon is a trademark of Penguin Random House LLC. Manufactured in China.

Library of Congress Cataloging-in-Publication Data is available.

ISBN 9780515157635   10 9 8 7 6 5 4 3 2 1